RAINBOW MIST SCHOOL
CLASS GOLDEN FEATHER

My name is: ......Comet......

My best friend is: ......My twin sister, Destiny...

My favourite colour is: ......Purple............

My favourite food is: ......Hay............

...I like to look after......

...my sister............

RAINBOW MIST SCHOOL
CLASS GOLDEN FEATHER

My name is: ......Destiny............

My best friend is: ......My twin brother, Comet

My favourite colour is: All the colours of the rainbow

My favourite food is: ......Grass............

...I like to do dares and...

...get into mischief!...

Sue Bentley's books for children often include animals, fairies and wildlife. She lives in Northampton and enjoys reading, going to the cinema and watching the birds on the feeders outside her window. She loves horses, which she thinks are all completely magical. One of her favourite books is *Black Beauty*, which she must have read at least ten times. At school she was always getting told off for daydreaming, but she now knows that she was storing up ideas for when she became a writer. Sue has met and owned many animals, but the wild creatures in her life hold a special place in her heart.

Sue Bentley

Magic Ponies

Seaside Summer

Illustrated by Angela Swan

PUFFIN

To Ginger – plucky brave little friend

PUFFIN BOOKS

Published by the Penguin Group
Penguin Books Ltd, 80 Strand, London WC2R 0RL, England
Penguin Group (USA) Inc., 375 Hudson Street, New York, New York 10014, USA
Penguin Group (Canada), 90 Eglinton Avenue East, Suite 700, Toronto, Ontario, Canada M4P 2Y3
(a division of Pearson Penguin Canada Inc.)
Penguin Ireland, 25 St Stephen's Green, Dublin 2, Ireland (a division of Penguin Books Ltd)
Penguin Group (Australia), 250 Camberwell Road, Camberwell, Victoria 3124, Australia
(a division of Pearson Australia Group Pty Ltd)
Penguin Books India Pvt Ltd, 11 Community Centre, Panchsheel Park, New Delhi – 110 017, India
Penguin Group (NZ), 67 Apollo Drive, Rosedale, North Shore 0632, New Zealand
(a division of Pearson New Zealand Ltd)
Penguin Books (South Africa) (Pty) Ltd, 24 Sturdee Avenue, Rosebank,
Johannesburg 2196, South Africa

Penguin Books Ltd, Registered Offices: 80 Strand, London WC2R 0RL, England

puffinbooks.com

First published 2009
1

Text copyright © Sue Bentley, 2009
Illustrations copyright © Angela Swan, 2009
All rights reserved

The moral right of the author and illustrator has been asserted

Set in Bembo
Made and printed in England by Clays Ltd, St Ives plc

British Library Cataloguing in Publication Data
A CIP catalogue record for this book is available from the British Library

ISBN: 978-0-141-32597-2

www.greenpenguin.co.uk

Prologue

The young magic pony folded his gold-feathered wings as he soared downwards towards Rainbow Mist Island. Moments later Comet's hooves landed on a stretch of shining pebble beach. It felt good to be home.

His tummy felt full of butterflies as he hoped that Destiny had found her way home at last. Comet's twin sister had been

lost for so long. He was looking forward
to finding her safe among their family of
Lightning Horses.

Tossing his head, so that his golden
mane fell forward on to his cream neck,
the magic pony trotted away from the sea
and headed up the steep hillside.

He reached the top and stood looking
down towards the familiar rolling plains
and forests. In the distance were the
mountains, wreathed in the shimmering,
multicoloured mist that gave the island
its name.

A warm breeze rippled through the
silvery grass, bringing the scent of fresh
water towards the magic pony. Comet's
deep violet eyes gleamed and he snorted
thirstily as he galloped down a slope.

Sunlight flashed on his smooth pale-cream coat and golden silky mane and tail. He reached the spring that trickled over some stones into a small pool and bent his head to drink.

A movement flickered over the nearby rocks and Comet saw the shadow of a large horse in the rippling water.

The magic pony threw up his head, his eyes rolling in alarm. Was this another Lightning Horse or one of the dark horses, who wanted to steal his magic? His pulse quickened as he slowly turned round.

An older horse with a wise expression and kind dark eyes stepped into view. 'Blaze!' Comet bent his head before the leader of the Lightning Herd.

'I am glad to see you again, Comet,' Blaze said warmly in a deep velvety neigh. 'Is Destiny with you?'

Comet felt a pang of bitter disappointment. 'No. I thought she must have found her way back safely by now.'

'I am afraid not. I do not think Destiny will return while she believes herself to be in terrible trouble for losing the Stone of Power,' Blaze told him regretfully.

The stone protected the Lightning Herd from the dark horses. Destiny had accidentally lost it when she and Comet were playing their favourite game of cloud-racing. Comet had found the stone, but Destiny had already fled.

'I wish I knew where Destiny was hiding.' Comet's proud arching neck drooped sadly.

'The stone will help us to find her.' Blaze pawed at the ground with one shining hoof. A fire-opal, glinting with many colours, appeared. As Comet and Blaze looked deeply into it, the stone grew larger and an image appeared in its shimmering depths.

Comet saw his twin sister galloping along the sandy shore of a place in a far-off world. 'Destiny!'

'She is alone and in danger,' Blaze said. 'You must go and find her before the dark horses discover where she is!'

There was a flash of bright violet light and a rainbow mist appeared around Comet. The light-cream pony with his golden wings disappeared and in his place stood a handsome pony with a white coat covered with black spots, a white mane and tail, and large deep violet eyes.

Comet snorted with decision. 'I will

use this disguise to search for Destiny!'

'Go now,' urged Blaze, nodding. 'There is no time to lose. Bring her back safely!'

'I will!' Comet vowed.

He neighed softly as violet sparkles ignited in his spotted coat and he felt the power building inside him. The rainbow mist swirled more thickly, twinkling as it drew Comet in.

Chapter
ONE

'Bye, thanks for visiting. Hope we'll see you again,' Jessie Starkling called politely as the last few kids and grown-ups climbed down from the carousel horses and wandered away across the fairground.

'That's the way, Jess. Number-one rule. Always leave the customers happy. That way, they're sure to come back!' her dad said, smiling.

Jess smiled back at him. It had been a long day helping out on the merry-go-round and she felt hot and tired. Tossing back her plait of glossy dark hair, she began flipping the controls that shut off the merry-go-round's hundreds of lights.

Her dad was already counting the day's takings. He was the youngest of the three brothers who owned and ran the

Starkling Brothers' Circus.

'One day you'll be running the fair. Looking after all the rides, just like me,' Mr Starkling said to his daughter.

'Yeah! In about a million years!' Jess's fourteen-year-old cousin, Mai, teased. She was tall with the same chocolate-brown eyes and glossy dark hair as Jess, but Mai's was shoulder length with a fringe. Her dad was the oldest of the Starkling brothers. She often lent an extra hand with the merry-go-round at busy times in the fairground.

'Says you! I might only be nine, but everyone knows kids grow up quickly in the circus!' Jess countered, her eyes sparkling.

Her dad nodded agreement. 'You certainly know all there is to know about this beauty,' he said, making a sweeping gesture with both arms at the beautiful merry-go-round.

Jess felt a surge of pride. She loved the carousel, which was well over a hundred years old. It had a double row of twenty-four galloping horses and each bit of it was covered with gilded carvings and tiny sparkling mirrors.

Jess adored every single one of the beautiful painted and gilded horses. She didn't mind all the work it took to keep them shiny and bright. But she also had a secret that not even Mai knew about.

Her dearest wish in the whole world was to have a real pony of her own.

Jess swallowed a sigh as she unlocked a cupboard in the central pillar and reached for the night covers for the rides. What was the point of wanting what you

couldn't have? The only horses allowed
on site were those in the bareback act,
which performed in the big top.

'Penny for them?' Mai said. 'You've got
that glassy-eyed look again. What are you
thinking about?'

'Oh, nothing much,' Jess said evasively.

Her dad was locking the cash box. 'I'm
going to skip off now,' he told the girls.
'There's a meeting in the big top, after the
evening performance. See you both later.'

'OK,' Jess said. She was used to shutting
the ride down for the night and could
do it with her eyes closed. 'Do you know
what the meeting's about?' she asked her
cousin as her dad moved away.

Mai shrugged. 'Probably about the
new site for next summer. It's all anyone's
talking about.'

Jess nodded. The news was all round
the circus. The site at Treen-on-Sea,
which had been the summer home of
the Starkling Brothers' Circus for the
last thirty-five years, was being sold
and a new housing estate built on it. It
had been a major shock to everyone,
including Jess.

'Why don't you go and find out what's
going on?' she suggested to her cousin.

'I'll finish up here and then follow you.'

Mai looked tempted, but she hesitated.
'Sure you'll be OK by yourself?'

Jess widened her brown eyes and gave
her cousin an 'are you kidding?' look.
She was related to virtually every person
around here. There was nowhere on earth
where she was safer!

Mai laughed and gave in. 'Right then.
Thanks, Jess. You're a star!'

As soon as she was alone, Jess picked
up a soft cloth and began happily wiping
down the carousel horses. She did this
every night without fail, even when the
horses didn't need it. They were all so
handsome, with their different-coloured
manes and tails, and brightly painted
saddles.

But one of them was Jess's special favourite.

It was a prancing white horse with black spots all over it like a Dalmatian dog. It had pricked ears, a particularly sweet face with realistic glass eyes, and blue-and-green trappings with gold highlights.

Jess ran her hand over the high-arched wooden neck and flowing mane and tail. A stir of longing swept through her as she wished she could have a pony just like this one. On impulse she mounted it and then put her feet in the stirrups. Reaching forward, she patted the glossy wooden neck.

'Well, horsey. How do you fancy going for a midnight ride? Just you and me,' she said softly, laughing at the very idea.

Suddenly there was a bright violet flash, and a thick glittering rainbow mist

crystal drops settling on her skin,
sparkling in the lights of the fairground.

'Oh!' She blinked, trying to see
through the strange mist.

As it slowly cleared, Jess felt a tremor
beneath her palm and the carousel
horse shook its head. Swishing its tail, it

straightened its legs and placed its four shining hooves firmly on the wooden platform.

'Hold tight, please!' it said in a velvety neigh.

Chapter
TWO

Jess almost fell off sideways in shock.
What was happening? She must be so
tired out after the busy evening that she
was light-headed! Carousel horses didn't
move and they certainly couldn't speak.

Before she had time to gather her
thoughts, the spotted pony sprang forward
in a mighty leap that cleared the carousel
horse in front and landed a few metres

away on the grass.

'Oh!' Jess gasped, clinging on tight with trembling fingers.

Somehow she kept her balance by sitting down firmly and gripping tightly with her legs. She wrapped her hands in the spotted pony's thick flowing white mane as it galloped across the fairground, weaving between the other rides and stalls in a dizzying burst of speed.

There was a strange tingling feeling flowing to the ends of Jess's fingers and bright violet sparks glinted in the pony's spotted coat. It was weird, but she felt quite safe, however fast they were going. In no time at all, they reached the edge of the fairground and came to a halt behind the big waltzer, which was dark and closed up for the night.

'Please get down now,' the pony whinnied gently.

Jess did so, still having trouble taking it all in. The moment her feet touched the ground, her legs started shaking and she almost sank to her knees.

The spotted pony quickly positioned itself so that she could lean against its strong shoulder. As Jess touched the warm silky skin, she felt herself starting to calm down.

'I am sorry if I frightened you,' the spotted pony whinnied apologetically. 'My name is Comet of the Lightning Herd. What is your name?'

Jess blinked at him. The amazing pony was breathing warm air through his nostrils in a friendly manner. To her surprise, she saw that he had glowing deep violet eyes.

'I'm J-J-Jessie. Jessie S-S-Starkling,' she stammered. 'But everyone calls me Jess. My dad and his two brothers own this circus.'

The pony bent his neck in a formal bow. 'I am honoured to meet you, Jess.'

'Um . . . me too.' Jess's curiosity was working overtime. 'I don't get it. What just happened? One minute you were a carousel horse and now you're real *and* you can talk! That's never happened before.'

'All of the Lightning Herd can talk. I live with them on Rainbow Mist Island, but I have come here to search for my twin sister, Destiny. I saw the moving machine with all the wooden horses and it seemed like a good place to hide. When you climbed on to my back, you took me by surprise.'

Jess grinned. 'Tell me about it! I think we *both* had quite a shock!'

Comet tossed his head in agreement, his bright eyes sparkling with amusement.

'Is Destiny one of the carousel horses too?' Jess wanted to know.

'No. She is lost somewhere nearby in this world.'

Jess nodded slowly. 'But why did Destiny come here in the first place?'

Concern flickered across Comet's spotted face. 'My twin sister thinks she is responsible for losing the Stone of Power that protects our herd from our enemies,' he explained. 'She lost it during one of our games of cloud-racing. I soon found the stone, but Destiny thought she was in terrible trouble and had already fled. Now she is in danger from the dark horses who would like to steal her magic.'

Jess listened hard. It all sounded so strange and wonderful. One thing in particular puzzled her. 'Cloud-racing? How . . .?'

Comet backed away slowly. 'Please stay there,' he ordered.

Jess felt another warm prickling sensation flow to the tips of her fingers as violet-coloured sparkles bloomed in Comet's white-and-black coat and more of the glittering rainbow mist rippled round him. The handsome spotted pony disappeared and in its place stood a majestic cream-coloured pony, with a proudly arched neck and a flowing golden mane and tail. Springing from his shoulders were magnificent wings, covered with glowing bright golden feathers.

Jess was totally speechless. She had never seen anything so beautiful in her whole life.

'Comet? Is . . . is that still you?' she gulped when she had regained her voice.

'Yes, Jess. This is my true form. Do not be afraid.' Comet gave a soft musical whinny. There was a final swirl of the magical sparkling mist and Comet instantly reappeared as a white-and-black spotted pony with a white mane and tail.

'Wow! That's a great disguise. Is Destiny hiding as a normal pony too?' Jess asked.

'Yes. She will also be in disguise, but that will not save her if the dark horses discover her,' Comet told her seriously. 'I must start looking for her. Will you help me?'

Jess saw that his beautiful, deep violet eyes were shadowed by sadness. He must be missing his twin sister. Her soft heart went out to the lonely magic pony.

'Of course I'll help you. We'll search for Destiny together!'

'Thank you, Jess.' Comet stepped forward and pushed his satiny nose into her cupped hands.

Jess stroked him, totally charmed. 'I can't wait to tell Mai about this. She's my older cousin and thinks she's really grown up, but she's brilliant –'

'No!' Comet lifted his head. 'I am sorry, Jess, but you can tell no one about me or what I have told you.'

Jess felt disappointed that she couldn't even tell Mai. It would have been great to share such a wonderful secret with her cousin.

'You must promise,' Comet neighed seriously, looking into her face with his intelligent eyes.

Jess nodded slowly. If it would help protect his twin sister from the dark horses until Comet could find her, she was prepared to agree. She knew how she would feel if Mai was ever to go missing. 'OK. I promise. Cross my heart.'

'Thank you, Jess.'

Jess smiled at him and reached up to pat his satiny spotted cheek. She had another thought. 'Where are you going to stay? The only ponies allowed on the site are those that perform in the circus.'

Comet tossed his head. 'I will hide as a carousel horse again.'

'But ... how's that going to work?' Jess asked. 'Customers will want to ride on you when the merry-go-round's working. Won't it be difficult for you to stay really still all the time?'

'I do not mind if people ride me on the big machine. It will be fun,' Comet told her, swishing his flowing tail. 'And I will use my magic, so that only you will see and hear me. Everyone else will just see a carved wooden horse.'

'Cool!' Jess exclaimed. 'The circus and fairground is closed in the daytime on weekdays, so we'll have loads of time to go out looking for Destiny together.'

Comet nodded, his eyes lighting up at the thought of finding his twin sister.

'We'd better go back now, before someone notices that one of the carousel horses is missing,' Jess reasoned. 'Besides, Mai will be wondering why I'm taking so long to close up for the night.'

'Very well. Climb on to my back again,' Comet invited.

Jess felt a surge of excitement as she mounted him and wrapped her hands in his mane. There was a final flash of violet light, visible only to Jess, as Comet shot forward. In no time at all, she was sitting on the merry-go-round, riding what appeared to be a normal spotted carousel horse.

'See you later!' she whispered as she gave Comet a hug before carefully sliding down and putting the canvas cover over him.

She only just managed to stop herself laughing aloud with happiness. Her dream, of having a pony of her own, had come true! But in a way she could never have imagined – not even in her wildest dreams!

Chapter
THREE

'I can't believe that Uncle Felix wants
to leave the circus!' Mai exclaimed as
she poked her head in through the open
caravan door early the following morning.
'How can he even think of staying put
somewhere and getting a normal job?'

Jess was just sitting down to eat her
breakfast. She'd had a brilliant dream
about flying through the air on Comet.

It had felt so real, even down to the
softness of his warm gold-feathered
wings, brushing against her. The
wonderful images still filled her mind.

'Um . . . yeah. That's too awful to think
about.' Jess forced herself to concentrate
on what her cousin was saying. 'Maybe
Uncle Felix didn't mean it, about leaving.'

Jess's mum smiled at Mai. 'Come on
in. You can't talk about this stuff on an
empty stomach. We're having scrambled
eggs. There's plenty for one extra.'

Mai smiled despite herself. 'Thanks, Aunt Lily.' Still looking worried, Mai took a plate from her aunt and sat down next to Jess.

'So how come you took so long to shut everything away last night, anyway?' Mai asked, chewing thoughtfully. 'You were ages.'

Jess was taken by surprise. There had been so many people in the big top, all talking at once, that she hadn't realized Mai had noticed that she was late. 'I . . . um, got chatting with . . . someone,' she replied vaguely. *You wouldn't believe who it was, even if I could tell you!* she thought. 'What did they say at the meeting?'

'Well.' Her mum spoke first. 'New houses are going up everywhere. There's not much open land left. I'm afraid that your dad thinks Felix has a point.'

Jess realized with a little jolt of dismay that her mum looked really worried. This was serious. Surely her dad wouldn't leave the circus!

She looked at Mai. 'What does Uncle Oliver say?' she asked her cousin.

'Dad's dead against quitting. He reckons the circus is in our blood! I'm with him. The Starklings have been circus people for generations. I'd rather die than do anything else!' she said fiercely.

Jess pushed her scrambled eggs around with a fork. Mai was always so dramatic, but this time Jess agreed with her. She couldn't think of anything worse than living in a normal house in a dull town, instead of travelling to the coast every summer and spending the season there.

They finished eating in thoughtful silence. Mai thanked her aunt for the food and then she and Jess helped clear away the dishes before they went off to do their chores.

'I'm litter-picking today. Bor-ing!' Mai said, rolling her eyes. 'At least I can listen to music while I do it. See you later!' She plugged in her headset as she wandered away.

Jess waved to her and then made her way to the temporary stables, where the troop of six handsome circus horses lived during the season. One of them, Samson, a large grey, leaned his head over his stall and nudged at her pocket for the treats she usually brought him.

'Hey! Stop that, cheeky!' Jess said, laughing, fishing out a mint for him.

She helped with mucking out and then changed water buckets and filled hay nets. Usually she felt a twinge of sadness, desperately longing for a pony of her own.

But today she was in higher spirits. She might not yet *own* her own pony, but she now she had a gorgeous, secret magic pony to keep her company.

As soon as she'd finished, Jess hurried towards the merry-go-round. Quickly checking that no one was looking, she lifted Comet's cover and stowed it away out of sight.

Comet gave a whicker of welcome as he shook himself. 'Greetings, Jess!'

Jess stroked his silky spotted neck delightedly. 'Hi, Comet. We can go for a ride together now to see if we can find Destiny. I reckon we've got a few hours before anyone wonders where I am.'

Luckily he was one of the inner ring horses, so someone would have to look really closely to notice that one carousel horse was missing.

'Thank you, Jess. Climb on to my back.'

'But what if someone sees us?' she
asked worriedly,

'I will use my magic so no one will
see either of us while you are riding me.'
Comet pawed at the wooden boards with
one front hoof.

Jess mounted him and almost
immediately she felt a familiar tingling
feeling in her fingertips as Comet's
spotted coat twinkled with violet sparks
and a faint rainbow mist swirled around
them.

'Ready?' Comet neighed.

'Definitely!'

'Hold tight!' Comet rocked back on
to his hind legs and pawed the air before
soaring over the other carousel horses in
such a huge leap that it felt as if they were
flying.

Jess caught her breath with excitement
as they sped away. Comet was thrilling
to ride, so smooth and fast. His hooves
hardly seemed to touch the ground as he
raced onwards at the speed of light.

Jess crouched low on his back, moving in time to his powerful strides. She had never ridden a pony flat out before, but she didn't feel the tiniest bit afraid. Shining rainbows gleamed in Comet's flowing white mane as his magic spread over her, making her feel warm and safe.

Soon the circus and fairground were far behind them. Jess told Comet that it would be safe for them both to become visible now, as they were not likely to meet anyone she knew. The magic pony nodded and in a flash of sparkly violet magic it was done.

Jess pointed him towards a quiet, narrow road, lined on both sides with wild-rose hedges. Their sweet scent filled the air as they swept past. 'This leads to the beach and the cliff tops. From up there we'll be able to see for miles.'

Comet galloped on tirelessly. As the beach came in sight, he gradually slowed to a trot and then a walk.

They began crossing a short stretch of soft sand. The magic pony's head turned from side to side as his keen eyes searched for signs of Destiny. Jess kept a lookout too, but they saw no other ponies.

It was still early and the sun wasn't yet hot. One or two people were walking dogs and a few families with kids were building sandcastles. Jess knew that later on this quiet beach would be teaming with holidaymakers.

Nearer the shore, there was a long expanse of solid wet sand. The breakers came in with a shushing noise and cool white foam swirled round Comet's legs

as he high-stepped along. With a neigh
of pleasure he sped up, kicking up spray
behind him as they rode on under a
cloudless blue sky.

Jess felt a glow of perfect happiness
spread through her chest. This had to
be the best thing ever – riding the most
amazing pony in the universe through the
shallow waves on a perfect day! She knew
she'd never forget it.

'The beach stretches on forever.
There are hundreds of caves in these cliffs,
and miles and miles of rough land on the
cliff tops. However will we find Destiny?'
she asked Comet.

The spotted pony twitched his silky
white tail. 'We have a special bond
because we are twins. If Destiny is close, I
will sense her presence. Also, wherever she
goes she will leave a trail.'

'A trail? What will it look like?' Jess
asked.

'There will be softly glowing hoof-
prints, which are invisible to most people
in this world.'

'Wow!' Jess said, fascinated. 'Will I be
able to see them?'

'Yes. If you are riding me or I am very
close to you,' Comet told her. A flicker of

excitement passed over his spotted skin
and he stretched his neck to peer up the
beach, where a line of ponies were just
emerging from a path down the hill.

Jess had seen them too. 'Do you
think that one of those ponies might be
Destiny? Let's go and see!'

Chapter
FOUR

Jess rose to the trot as Comet's hooves drummed on the packed sand and he closed the distance between himself and the other ponies.

She could see now that there were five of them. Four were being ridden by small children, with an older girl on a stocky chestnut mare leading the group. She smiled and waved when she saw Jess

approaching.

Jess felt encouraged by the girl's friendly expression. 'Hi! Lovely day for riding, isn't it?' she called out, as she and Comet drew level with the riders.

'Yeah! Just perfect,' the girl said, slowing her chestnut mare. Behind her, the young riders reined in their ponies 'Take five, everyone. We'll give the ponies a short rest,' she said to them with a smile.

Comet whinnied and gave a friendly blow as he looked closely at the five ponies. They, in turn, tossed their heads and flicked their ears forward. One or two nickered back and Jess's heart leapt with hope for her magical friend.

But Comet turned away in disappointment, his head drooping. None of them was Destiny. Jess realized that it wasn't going to be so simple to find her. She could tell that her magic pony was worried about his twin sister, who was lost and all alone.

'We'll keep searching. And we won't stop until we find Destiny,' she promised him in a whisper, patting his silky neck.

'Thank you, Jess,' Comet neighed softly.

The girl on the chestnut mare looked at Jess curiously. 'I'm Ellen. Ellen Bridgemore.' She looked about twelve years old and had short fair hair and a round pretty face. 'I often bring rides down on to the beach, but I haven't seen you around here before.'

'Um . . . no. I've only just got Comet,' Jess said. It wasn't exactly a fib, because Comet *had* only just chosen her to be his friend. 'It's the first time I've been out on a long ride with him. I'm Jessie Starkling, by the way. But everyone calls me Jess.'

'Wow! Your first proper ride? That's exciting for you both,' Ellen enthused. 'It's great fun working with a new pony and getting to know him, isn't it? Comet's gorgeous. Such unusual spotted markings.'

'Yes. Comet's *very* unusual, all right,' Jess said, biting back a grin. She wondered what Ellen would have said if she knew how special Comet really was! 'Your pony's lovely too. What's her name?' she asked.

Ellen's chestnut pony had a glossy coat. Its face was slightly dished, with a gentle expression and large dark eyes.

'Bliss,' Ellen told her. 'She's my favourite, although I love all our ponies. Bliss is so steady and good-natured. She'd lead the ride back home even if I fell asleep in the saddle! My mum owns a riding stable in Lower Treen,' she explained.

'Really?' Jess said. 'It must be hard work looking after all those ponies.'

Ellen nodded. 'You bet. But we're not as busy as we used to be.' A shadow of worry flickered across her face. 'A posh new riding stable has just opened up down the coast and some of our customers have started going there. There's only Mum and me, so I usually

help out after school and at weekends and
school holidays, like now. There's nothing
else I'd rather be doing. Ponies rule, right?
That's what I always say –' She stopped
as she seemed to realize that Jess couldn't
get a word in edgeways. 'Sorry!' she said,
grinning ruefully. 'Once I start on about

ponies and riding I can go on all day.
Mum says she's going to get me fitted
with a "pause" button!'

'That's OK. I like it,' Jess said, grinning.
'Pony talk is my favourite thing! But I
don't know anyone who's as mad about
ponies as me!'

'You do now!' Ellen joked.

They both laughed.

Jess was enjoying herself. She hoped
that she and Ellen might get to know
each other better. It was great having
Comet as her secret friend, but she
couldn't ever let anyone at the circus see
him or tell them how wonderful he was.
It would be good fun to have a brand-
new horsey friend to go riding with.

'I've always loved everything about
ponies and horses,' Jess told Ellen.

'I wanted one of my own for ages . . . and then Comet suddenly appeared . . . um, I mean, came along,' she corrected quickly. 'Before I got him, I never went for any long rides. I help look after the circus horses, so I was allowed to ride one of them sometimes, but only on site.'

Ellen's eyes widened. 'Circus . . .? Oh, you're Jess *Starkling*! I thought I recognized the name. So your family *owns* the circus. Mum and Dad took me to see a show there once. Wow! That's so cool. It must be an exciting life.'

Jess felt herself blushing. She shrugged. 'I guess so. I'm used to it.'

Ellen suddenly noticed that the young riders with her were fidgeting impatiently. She gave them an apologetic grin. 'Sorry, guys. You didn't come on a ride to hear

me waffling on! Why don't you go down
to the shore? You can ride along in the
shallows. But don't go any faster than a
trot and turn back when you get to the
Needle, OK?' she said, pointing to a tall
rock formation that was visible in the
near distance.

'Can I lead, Jess?' a brown-haired boy
on a fat little bay pony piped up eagerly.

Ellen nodded. 'Fine with me, Ross.
You're a confident rider, and you're used
to Sparky.'

Ross squared his shoulders and sat up straight. 'Follow me, everyone!' he said proudly, urging his pony forward. The others followed, heading down to the patch of packed wet sand and the rolling breakers.

'Ellen's nice, isn't she?' Jess whispered to Comet, while the older girl was distracted. 'Do you mind if I stay and chat to her for a while?'

'I would like that. Bliss is a fine pony too,' he whinnied good-naturedly.

'Thanks, Comet. You're the best!' Jess said, feeling a surge of affection for him.

After the young riders had bounced away on their ponies, Ellen turned back to Jess. 'So – tell me what it's like to live in a circus. And don't miss anything out!' she joked.

Jess grinned. 'This could take a *really* long time!'

While Jess and Ellen chatted, Comet and Bliss breathed in each other's scent and then gently touched noses, making friends in their own pony way.

Deep in conversation, the girls hardly noticed the next few minutes passing, but eventually Ellen checked her wristwatch.

'I'd better go and meet those kids and head back to the stables with them. Their parents will soon be back at the yard waiting to pick them up. Mum doesn't like to keep people waiting. She says it's bad for business.'

Jess nodded. She knew all about keeping customers happy.

Ellen narrowed her eyes to peer at the shoreline in the distance. 'Here's Ross leading them back now,' she said, raising her arm to wave.

Suddenly warning shouts rang out, and a child's bright-orange dinghy came careering down to the seashore. One of the ponies reared in fright and leapt forward into the waves.

'Oh my goodness!' Jess gasped, as the young rider screamed and held on tightly as her pony plunged about in fear.

'Oh no! That's Lana on Pie!' Ellen cried. 'She's one of our newest riders!' Kicking Bliss on, she shot towards the commotion.

Jess was already racing after her on Comet, his white mane and tail streaming out behind him.

At the shore, Ross had halted his pony. 'Ellen! It wasn't my fault. That dinghy scared Pie. Now Lana can't get him to come back in,' the boy gulped, close to tears.

'It's OK, Ross. I saw what happened. I'll get Pie. The rest of you stay here,' Ellen ordered. 'The sea gets deeper just a few metres out.'

She kicked Bliss on, urging the chestnut into the water. But her usually calm pony hesitated, rolling her eyes and dancing sideways.

'Bliss can feel the current pulling against her legs,' Comet neighed worriedly.

'It must be even stronger where Lana is,' Jess guessed. 'She and Pie could get swept right out!'

Further out, Lana seemed frozen with terror as she clutched tight to Pie's

neck. 'Hold on!' Ellen called to her. 'I'll
get help.' She turned Bliss and rode her
back on to the beach. 'Has anyone got a
mobile? We have to call the coastguard!'
she said in a shaky voice.

The other young riders shook their
head. 'There might be a phone box at the
beach cafe,' one of them said.

'There is no time to waste!' Comet
whinnied. 'Are you ready, Jess?'

'Go for it!' Jess told him in a low voice. 'Don't worry, Ellen. We'll get the coastguard!' she said more loudly.

She felt a warm prickling sensation flowing down to the ends of her fingertips as bright violet sparks ignited in Comet's spotted coat and tiny rainbows flashed in his silky white mane and tail.

Something very strange was about to happen!

Chapter
FIVE

The magic pony gave a determined snort
and time seemed to stand still.

In what seemed like slow motion
Comet leapt into the waves, trailing
invisible sparks like a shooting star. At
the same time a thick mist settled over
the sea, hiding them from Ellen and the
others waiting on the shore.

'Hold tight!' Comet warned Jess.

Jess kept her seat as he galloped
effortlessly through the deeper waves.
Freezing seawater lapped against her,
soaking her to the waist, but Comet's
sparkly magic somehow kept her warm.

Lana's terrified pony was panicking.
The thick mist seemed like another scary
thing to be afraid of. With a shrill cry,
it backed up and then spun round as it
battled against the treacherous current.

'Hurry, Comet!' Jess urged. 'Lana's only
just hanging on!'

Comet opened his mouth and breathed out a whoosh of violet sparkles, which sprinkled around the other pony like fine rain. For a moment, Pie seemed to grow calmer. The pony stopped plunging about and stood waiting for Comet to reach it – until a particularly large wave washed the sparkles away.

Without Comet's calming magical influence, Pie kicked out strongly again. The current caught the pony and brought it surging straight at Comet and Jess. Jess gasped as Pie's flailing hooves seemed about to slam into Comet.

She didn't think twice. Leaning forward, she stretched out her arm.

Almost . . . almost. Yes!

'Got you!' Jess's fingers closed on Pie's wet mane and she managed to hold the pony at arm's length, but then gasped in pain as her arm was twisted at an angle. Gritting her teeth, she held on tight. 'It's OK, Lana. You're safe now!' she called to the shivering little girl.

Lana didn't answer. She had her eyes tightly closed and kept them shut, while Comet towed her and Pie to shore. As Comet splashed through the shallows with Pie and Lana, every last bright spark faded from his spotted coat. The thick mist dissolved into strands and instantly disappeared.

The moment they all reached firm sand, Comet came to a halt. Jess finally let go of Pie's wet mane, relieved to be able to ease her aching arm.

Ellen had dismounted. She rushed forward, grabbed the pony's bridle and then put her jacket round Lana's shoulders.

The other young riders cheered and clapped. 'Way to go, Comet!' Ross yelled.

'Are you OK?' Ellen asked Lana worriedly.

Lana nodded. Her cheeks were now flushed and she seemed to be enjoying being the centre of attention. 'It was really exciting! I wasn't scared a bit!'

Ellen gave her a rather wobbly smile and then turned to Jess. 'Thanks so much,

Jess. And thanks to you too, Comet,' she said, patting his neck.

'You are welcome,' Comet neighed, but of course Ellen heard only normal pony noises.

'I feel awful. I should have kept a closer eye on everyone,' Ellen said guiltily. 'You couldn't have known that dinghy would blow across the beach and scare Pie,' Jess comforted. 'Anyway, no one's been hurt.'

Ellen nodded. 'I guess not. Hopefully Mum will be able to smooth things over with Lana's parents. We can't afford to lose any more customers.' She paused and looked thoughtful. 'That freaky mist was odd, wasn't it? It seemed to come out of nowhere.'

'Um . . . yeah. Strange. Anyway, glad we could help,' Jess said. She suddenly

realized how late it must be. She needed
to get back to the circus before she was
missed. The last thing she wanted was
for someone to mount a full-scale search
party! 'I've gotta go now! Maybe I'll see
you here again?'

'Definitely. And come by and say hello,
if you're ever passing Bridgemore Stables,'
Ellen said. 'You can't miss us. We're the
first place you come to in the village.'

'Thanks. I will,' Jess said, meaning
it. She'd love to meet up with Ellen
sometime.

She and Comet made their way
back along the beach. Now that the
excitement was over, Jess's injured arm
began throbbing. She winced at its
soreness.

'You hurt yourself when you stopped

Lana's pony kicking me,' Comet neighed in concern. 'Let me make you better. Get down for moment, please.'

Jess dismounted awkwardly, trying not to jar her bad arm. The magic pony turned his head and blew out a big warm breath that twinkled with thousands of tiny sparkling violet stars. There was a faint crackling sound as the glittery mist surrounded her arm and then sank into it and disappeared. The pain increased for a second and then melted away, just as if it was sand pouring out of a bucket.

'I feel fine again now. Thanks, Comet.'

He bent his head and gently nuzzled her shoulder. She reached up and leaned against his warm cheek. 'We didn't get a chance to go and look along the cliff path, did we? Next time we go out

looking for Destiny, we'll do that. And
maybe we'll look in at Bridgemore
Stables?'

Comet tossed his head in agreement.

Chapter
SIX

As evening fell, the fairground came to life. Coloured lights flashed cheerfully, jaunty organ music rang out, and the delicious smells of toffee apples, candyfloss and hamburgers rose on the air.

Jess loved this time of day, just before night fell. The place had a fairy-tale atmosphere.

From where she stood at the centre of

the merry-go-round, she could see the
queue building up outside the big top.
Inside, the performers would be ready
for the show. The troop of horses was
perfectly groomed and the clowns were
in their gaudy costumes.

Her dad was busily helping people get
on to the steps up to the merry-go-round
and mount the painted horses. Once all
the customers were ready, Mr Starkling
gave Jess the signal to start and she pulled
the lever.

The merry-go-round began to move, slowly at first and then turning faster and faster, its shiny gilt carvings and small mirrors flashing in the bright lights. Jess smiled at the carousel horses prancing up and down on their poles as they whirled past in time to the jaunty organ music.

A mother and her small child sat astride Comet. The child was laughing and clapping his pudgy little hands with glee. The magic pony tossed his head and whinnied with enjoyment.

'This is fun!' he neighed.

Jess smiled to herself. It had taken her a while to get used to the fact that she was the only person who could see that Comet was a real living, breathing pony. She wished she could talk properly to him, but there was barely time between customers to whisper a quick word.

It was a busy couple of hours and Jess was glad when Mai came to lend a hand. 'How's it going?' her cousin asked, expertly leaping aboard the spinning ride and weaving her way towards Jess.

'Good. It's been non-stop so far,' Jess replied.

'I noticed,' Mai said, reaching out and patting Comet's smooth spotted wooden back. 'This horse is suddenly very popular. Everyone seems to want to ride on it.'

'Really?' Jess said innocently. 'I wonder why?' *It looks like people somehow sense that Comet's special, without knowing why*, she thought.

'I'm going to grab a coffee, now that you're here, Mai. I'll be back in twenty minutes. Do you girls want anything?' Mr

Starkling asked.

'Not for me, thanks,' Mai said brightly.

'I'm OK. I'll get a drink later,' Jess said.

Both girls watched Jess's dad walk away. Mai turned back to Jess. 'Where did you disappear to this morning? I looked for you after I finished litter-picking.'

'I went to the beach,' Jess said truthfully.

Mai raised her eyebrows. 'By yourself?'

'Yeah. I . . . um, fancied a walk.'

Mai wrinkled her nose in amusement. 'Walk? You're weird.'

Jess laughed. 'I met a girl called Ellen. She was leading some kids on ponies. Her mum owns a riding stable in Lower Treen. She was really nice. You'd like her. Maybe you'll meet her sometime.'

Mai shrugged. 'It hardly seems worth it,' she commented. 'We'll soon be packing

up and leaving and we'll probably never
come back here.'

Jess felt a stab of sadness as she realized
that her cousin was right. It didn't seem
possible that their way of life may have to
change forever. She was sure that a perfect
summer site must be somewhere – it was
just a matter of finding it.

Mai operated the merry-go-round
controls as the ride came to an end. The
carousel horses slid to a halt and Jess

helped a small boy and girl and their
grandma climb down. The rest of the
customers drifted away.

Comet turned his head and gave a
friendly blow that ruffled her dark hair.
His deep violet eyes were glowing.

'You're doing great,' she whispered to
him, patting his silky neck.

When she looked up, she saw Mai
watching. Her cousin shook her head
slowly. 'Now you're *talking* to that spotted
horse! What is it with you?' Mai came
over and peered closely at Comet.

Jess had to try really hard not to burst
out laughing as her cousin waggled
her fingers and pulled silly faces, while
Comet blinked at her calmly and swished
his silky tail.

Finally Mai got bored and wandered

down to sit on the wooden steps that led
up to the carousel horses. Jess sat next to
her.

There was no one waiting for the
next ride. They could take it easy while
another queue gradually built up.

A group of four tough-looking teenage
boys appeared between the stalls, kicking
cans and laughing and nudging each
other. They narrowly missed jostling
a man with a toddler. The man spoke
sharply to them and got a mouthful of
cheek in reply.

'Uh-oh,' Jess groaned, sensing trouble
brewing.

'Oh, great,' Mai echoed, rolling her
eyes. 'I saw those pests messing about
earlier. They would turn up here, just
when Uncle Kit's gone for a break.'

'Maybe they'll just go past,' Jess said hopefully.

'Fat chance!' Mai sighed. 'Look out!'

Jess just had time to duck as one of the boys booted the can at the merry-go-round. It missed her by a couple of centimetres and clanged loudly against the carousel horse beside her.

'You idiot! You almost hit me!' she cried hotly.

The boys nudged each other and swaggered over. One of them, with short hair and a thin mean face under a navy-blue baseball cap, glared up at her. 'Who are you calling an idiot?' he sneered, putting his hands on his hips.

Jess swallowed. 'Who do you think?' she said, hoping she sounded braver than she felt.

One of the other boys called out. 'Are
you going to let her speak to you like
that, Liam?'

'Nah! Course not. She's going to make
it up to me!' Liam turned to Jess with
a challenging grin. 'Give us a free ride
then!'

Mai stepped forward. She squared her
shoulders. 'You wish! Push off, you lot.
Before I lose my temper!'

'Who's rattled your cage?' Liam
mocked.

The other boys sniggered. They
exchanged glances and then all four of
them rushed forward and clambered on
to a horse each.

'Go on then. Start up this heap of old
rust!' Liam ordered.

Mai folded her arms, the colour rising

into her cheeks. Jess watched helplessly as
the boys stood up and began leaping from
horse to horse and swinging round the
poles. Jess saw Liam preparing to jump on
to Comet.

Her lips twitched. *Big mistake*, she
thought. *Huge!*

Chapter
SEVEN

Jess watched as the tough boy landed on
Comet's back and began jumping up and
down. His trainers made a slapping sound
against the painted wooden saddle.

Comet gave an angry neigh and slowly
turned his head to look at the boy, but, of
course, only Jess could see this.

Suddenly Comet's deep violet eyes
flashed with mischief, and rainbow

sparkles twinkled in his mane. He
bunched his hindquarters, kicked out
strongly and gave a mighty buck.

'Argh!' Liam appeared to shoot high
into the air. He whizzed towards a waste
bin about five metres away and landed
backside first, getting jammed in the bin
with his legs and arms sticking up and
waggling helplessly. 'Help! I'm stuck!' he
wailed.

His friends jumped down and ran over.
Grabbing his arms and legs, they heaved

him out.

'Are you OK, bro?' asked one of them.

'What did you do that for?' another asked.

Liam scrambled to his feet, looking red-faced and shaken. 'I just felt like it, didn't I?' he bluffed, eyeing the carousel horses warily. 'That dumb merry-go-round's kids' stuff, anyway. I'm going on the dodgem cars,' he decided, slouching away.

'Hey! Wait for us!' The others hurried to catch up with him.

Mai scratched her head as she watched them go. 'I don't get it! What just happened?'

'Beats me,' Jess said innocently, grinning at Comet. 'I'm just glad they've cleared off. Oh, good. Here's Dad coming back.

I'll go and get us a cold drink.' She
scooted off, before Mai could ask her any
more awkward questions.

A few days later, Jess and Comet were
exploring the cliff path. Below them, the
sandy bay was visible in a wide curve.
Seagulls wheeled overhead.

There had been no sign of Destiny
or any other ponies and Comet was
becoming more downcast.

Jess halted Comet near an area where
the path widened. She took in the wide
sky, the deep folds and grassy slopes and
the headland with the Needle stretching
out to sea. The cliff path snaked across
the hills, leading into the valley and the
village of Lower Treen.

'I hoped we might bump into Ellen

again,' she said. 'Maybe she's taken the riders somewhere else today after that scare in the sea. I hope she didn't get into trouble with her mum or Lana's parents.'

Comet's long white mane lifted in the fresh sea breeze. 'I would like to see her and Bliss again,' he whinnied.

'Me too,' Jess said eagerly. 'We're not far from Bridgemore Stables. Shall we go there? We can keep a lookout for Destiny on the way.'

Comet snorted eagerly, pulling at his bit and springing forward.

Jess moved in time to his powerful strides, taking in big breaths of the clean salty air. She didn't think she'd ever get used to the wonderful sensation of riding the magic pony. There was no one about and she loved the feeling of freedom.

It was as if she and Comet were totally
alone in the whole wide world.

The cliff path gradually led downwards
and slopes of green hillside rose up on
either side of them. Comet's hooves
clattered as he stepped out on to the track
that led into the village.

Almost opposite, Jess spotted a large
red-brick building set back from the
road. Beside the gatepost there was a
sign with a rearing horse and the words
'Bridgemore Riding Stables'.

Jess turned Comet in through the gates

and they went towards the yard. She
could see Pie, Bliss and some other ponies
tethered outside. As they rode up, Ellen
came out. She was holding a body brush
and a curry comb.

The moment Ellen saw that the visitors
were Jess and Comet, her face lit up. 'Hi,
you two! I'm so glad you called in.'

'We've been exploring the cliffs,'
Jess told her, dismounting and holding
Comet's bridle. 'We thought we might see
you leading another ride.'

Ellen shook her head. 'I wish,' she
sighed. 'We've had more cancellations.
In fact, we've only got four bookings for
the whole day. I said I'd groom the spare
ponies, while Mum took the customers
out. I thought it might take her mind off
things. She's worried sick about trying to

keep the riding school going.'

'Oh, that's awful,' Jess sympathized. She remembered Ellen telling her that a posh new riding stable had opened up further along the coast. It looked as if things could only get worse for Ellen and her mum. 'Do you want a hand?' she offered. 'I'm used to grooming the circus ponies.'

Ellen nodded, cheering up a bit. 'OK. Thanks. It'll be more fun if we do it together.'

Jess tied Comet up next to Bliss. The chestnut pony gave a neigh of welcome and snuffled Comet's spotted neck.

'Aw, look at those two. Aren't they sweet!' Ellen crooned. 'Bliss's really taken with your spotted pony!'

Jess grinned. *Comet's irresistible all right!* she thought adoringly.

She filled a bucket of water so Comet
could have a drink, before starting work.
And for the next hour it was pony
pamper time. Jess picked out hooves,
brushed ponies' coats and combed out
manes and tails. Soon all the ponies
looked spick and span.

'Phew!' Jess swept a strand of dark hair
back from her sweaty forehead.

'Time for a drink and a snack! I think
we've earned it,' Ellen announced. She
led Jess into the large farmhouse-style
kitchen.

They sat at the wooden table with their
cold drinks and bags of crisps. Munching,
Jess looked out of the kitchen window.
She could see the village road that curved
past open fields and then back to the
coast. Sunlight glittered off the nearby

sea. 'What a brilliant view,' she said admiringly.

Ellen nodded. 'I love it here and I'd hate to move, but Mum says we might have to. She wants to improve the stables, so we can offer indoor schooling and stuff. So she's been trying to sell a field she owns just outside the village to get more money to be able to do it. But no one wants to buy, because it's no good for building houses on.'

'What a shame,' Jess said. 'Is it a big field?'

'Yeah, pretty big. You can see for yourself if you go back to the beach by road, instead of across the cliffs. It's got a "for sale" notice. Why?'

'Oh, just wondering,' Jess said. She was starting to tingle with excitement, as an idea began forming in her mind.

Chapter
EIGHT

The house phone rang as Jess was leaving
Ellen's kitchen for the stable yard.

'I'd better get that,' Ellen decided. 'It
might be a booking. Won't be a mo! I'll
catch you up.'

Comet gave a whicker of welcome
when he saw Jess. His intelligent eyes
twinkled at her as she untied him. Jess
felt her heart lift in response. Having the

magic pony for her friend was the best thing in the world.

Holding his bridle, Jess patted his silky spotted neck. 'Ellen's just told me that her mum owns a large field. It's got me thinking. We need somewhere for the circus for next year and she needs to make some money. Maybe we could help each other. What do you think?' she asked.

'Perhaps we should go and look at the field,' Comet snorted.

Jess nodded. 'Just what I thought. We can check it out on our way back!'

She glanced at her wristwatch, surprised to see that it was quite late in the afternoon. It wouldn't be long before the circus people began getting ready for the evening session. But there was just

time to look at the field if they hurried.

Ellen came striding towards them. She was holding the cordless house phone.

Jess took one look at the older girl's face. 'Problem?' she guessed.

'And then some,' Ellen groaned. 'That was Mrs Penrose. Her daughter, Kay, is one of our regular riders. Apparently Kay was wearing an expensive necklace yesterday and somehow lost it on the ride. Mrs Penrose is furious. She says Kay won't be coming here again *and* she wants Mum to pay for a new necklace.'

'Oh, no,' Jess sympathized. She couldn't believe that this was happening to Ellen and her mum on top of everything else. 'But how come it's your fault, if Kay lost it? No one wears an expensive necklace to go riding.'

'Try telling Mrs Penrose that,' Ellen said glumly, looking close to tears. 'I saw Kay when she arrived. And I'm sure she wasn't wearing a necklace or I would have asked her to leave it in one of the lockers for customers' valuables.' She sighed as she lifted the phone, ready to punch in a number. 'I'd better call Mum on her mobile. She's not going to believe this.'

Comet pricked his ears. 'Please tell

Ellen to wait, Jess,' he neighed.

Jess blinked, wondering what he was up to. But she trusted her magical friend's judgement. 'Ellen! Don't tell her yet!' she said quickly. 'Can you wait until she gets back?'

Ellen lowered the phone, frowning. 'I guess so. But if you're thinking of going to look for the necklace, I wouldn't bother. It'll be like trying to find a needle in about ten haystacks.'

Jess grinned. She wished she could tell Ellen that she had a big advantage. Comet! 'Trust me. Everything's going to be fine! I'll be back as soon as I can!' she said reassuringly.

Ellen didn't look convinced, but she nodded and managed a worried grin.

The moment they were out of sight of

the riding stable, Comet slipped behind
a tall hedge. Jess felt a familiar tingling
sensation flowing down to the ends of her
fingertips and violet sparkles glinted in
the magic pony's spotted coat. They were
brighter than she'd ever seen them and
they formed into a whirling tube shape,
which flashed with tiny rainbow glints.

Comet leapt forward into the tube and stood there without moving. The tube shape rippled, moving backwards past them. Jess saw blue skies and sunlight, then darkness and glinting stars. A rosy dawn flushed the magical tube with its glow and then it was daylight again and they were trotting along the cliff-top path.

A salty sea breeze ruffled Jess's dark hair and she could see the last strands of morning mist as they dissolved in the sun. 'Wow! You've taken us *back* to yesterday! That's amazing!' Jess exclaimed.

'No one will see us, Jess. My magic has made us invisible,' Comet told her.

In the distance she saw the line of riders, with Ellen's mum at the head of them on Bliss. Jess recognized Lana, Ross and the other young riders from the other day. A pretty girl she hadn't seen before was riding a black-and-white pony at the back of the group.

'That must be Kay Penrose,' she guessed. 'Let's get closer.'

Comet put on a spurt of speed. As they drew level with Kay, Jess saw the girl slip her hand inside the neck of her T-shirt. She drew out a gold chain with a sparkly heart on it.

'Stupid necklace! I wanted a pony charm bracelet!' Kay grumbled. Making sure that no one was looking, she threw the necklace into the air.

It glittered in the sunlight as it headed for the centre of a thorny bush. Comet moved with the speed of light, leaping high into the air and Jess reached out. Her fingers stretched to their limit. They

touched the chain. Yes! She caught the
necklace and folded it into her palm.

'Our work here is done,' Comet
neighed triumphantly as his shining
hooves touched down on to the grass.
He wheeled and set off back towards the
village.

'You're the best, Comet!' Jess cried.

She was reaching forward to pat him,
when she felt him stiffen and slow down.

He stopped and stood staring down at the grass. Jess looked down too.

In front of them and stretching away across the cliff top was a faint line of softly glowing violet hoof-prints.

'Destiny! She has been here!' Comet whinnied excitedly.

Jess felt a pang. Did that mean he was leaving, right now? 'Are . . . are you going after her?' she asked, her pulses racing.

Comet shook his head. 'No. The trail is cold. But it proves that Destiny was here yesterday,' he said, his eyes shining with new hope. 'When she is very close, I will be able to hear her hoof-beats. And then I may have to leave suddenly, without saying goodbye.'

Jess chewed at her lip as she realized that she'd been secretly hoping that he would stay forever. 'You could both stay here with me and hide as carousel horses,' she suggested.

'I am afraid that is not possible. We must return to our family on Rainbow Mist Island. Do you understand that, Jess?' Comet neighed gently.

Jess nodded, feeling her throat tighten with tears. 'I . . . I understand,' she said quietly, forcing herself to smile. She decided to try not to think about Comet leaving and to enjoy every single moment spent with him.

Chapter
NINE

The last magical violet sparkles faded as Jess and Comet emerged from the glittery tube, which had brought them back to the moment just after they'd left Ellen.

'Isn't magic wonderful?' Jess sang out happily. But it was more wonderful by far to have a magic pony all to herself!

Comet came out from behind the hedge and trotted towards the outskirts of Lower Treen.

'You're going the wrong way. The
stable's back there,' Jess cried.

'I thought you wanted to look at
the field Ellen's mother owns,' Comet
reminded her.

Jess nodded. 'Oh, yeah! Sorry. I was so
busy thinking about taking the necklace
back to Ellen that I almost forgot. What
would I do without you?'

They reached the edge of the village
and Jess soon spotted the empty field

with its 'for sale' sign. It was within easy distance of the seafront and was as flat and large as their present site.

Altogether it seemed perfect.

'I reckon the circus and fairground would easily fit on here! And there's room for our motorhomes and stuff. Maybe our horses could stay at Bridgemore Stables too,' she reasoned. 'Now all I have to do is tell Dad and the uncles. And they can talk to Ellen's mum.' She felt a moment of doubt. 'Do you think it will work? What if Uncle Felix still wants to leave the circus and my dad agrees with him? Maybe it will need more of your magic?'

'Magic cannot fix everything,' Comet told her gently. 'You have done all you can. Now you must leave it to the grown-ups to decide what to do.'

'You're right,' Jess said, smiling at her friend's wisdom. 'Let's take the necklace to Ellen, before we hurry back to the circus.'

Comet nickered agreement.

As the gateway to the riding stable came into view, Jess could see Ellen and her mum in the yard. They were helping to untack ponies and lead them into the loose boxes. The young riders had all gone and Jess guessed that their parents had collected them. Hopefully she'd be able to slip the necklace to Ellen without her mum noticing.

She was just about to ride into the yard when a familiar voice called out.

'Jess? Thank goodness!' Mai called, emerging from the track opposite. 'I've been up on the cliffs looking for you.

Everyone's worried sick. You've been
gone for ages. What are you doing here?
And how come you're riding that pony?'

Jess froze, her thoughts whirling. 'The
. . . um, riding stable wasn't that busy
today,' she said in a rush of inspiration. 'So
Ellen let me . . . um, borrow Comet. But
never mind that now. I've got some great
news. I think I've found a new summer
site for the circus!'

Mai listened as Jess quickly outlined
her idea about the empty field. 'It sounds
as if it could be what we're looking for,'
she said eagerly when Jess had finished.

'I think so too. But I don't know if Dad
and the uncles will go for it,' Jess mused.

'Well, here's your chance to ask them!'
Mai exclaimed.

A car zoomed to a halt and Jess's dad

and Uncle Oliver got out. Jess saw that her dad had a face like thunder. Her spirits sank into the ground.

'Oh, heck. I'm in so much trouble,' she whispered to Comet.

Comet gave a soft reassuring blow to show that he was on her side.

'Jess! Where on earth have you been? You know better than to go off without telling anyone,' her dad cried. 'It's a good thing Mai remembered you talking about these riding stables.'

'Sorry, Dad,' she said in a subdued voice. 'I didn't mean to be late. I lost track of time. But I've got something to tell you —'

'That can wait. Take that pony back, please,' her dad interrupted firmly. 'We're leaving, right now. You're grounded, young lady!'

Jess knew when her dad meant business. She sighed. Everything had suddenly got so complicated. She couldn't think what to say or do.

Comet decided for her. 'Pretend to take me back, Jess. You still need to give the necklace to Ellen,' he neighed, going towards the stable.

'OK,' Jess whispered to him glumly. She had no idea what was going to happen after that.

Behind them, she heard Mai talking. 'Dad! Uncle Kit! You have to listen to Jess. It's *really* important . . .'

As Jess rode into the yard, Ellen looked up and smiled. The tack-room door was open and Jess could see Ellen's mum inside.

Quickly dismounting, she fished the
necklace out of her pocket and held it
out to the older girl. 'I found it on the
cliffs,' she told her quietly. 'Kay threw it
away, because she really wanted a pony
charm bracelet.'

Ellen gaped at her. 'That's totally
amazing! Thanks a million, Jess. Now I
can phone Mrs Penrose with the good

news and Mum need never know. But
— how did you find out that Kay lost it
on purpose?'

Oops! Jess gulped. She shouldn't have
mentioned she knew that part. Ellen
would never believe the truth. 'I . . . um,
can sometimes tell fortunes and stuff. It's
a family thing!'

Ellen looked impressed and then a
puzzled expression came over her face.
'Who are those people by the gate?
They're looking up here and pointing.
Do you know them?'

'Yeah, that's my cousin, Mai, with her
dad, my Uncle Oliver. And the other
man's my dad. They came to find me
because I'd been gone for so long.' Just as
she finished speaking, Jess heard a sound
she'd been hoping for and dreading both

at the same time.

The hollow sound of galloping hooves overhead.

She froze. Destiny! There was no mistake. Comet gave an eager whinny and set off towards the back of the stable block, following the magical hoof-beats that were getting louder and closer.

Jess rushed after him. 'There's something I have to do! I'll be right back!' she called over her shoulder to Ellen.

As she rounded the building there was a flash, and a twinkling rainbow mist floated down around Comet. He stood there in his true form, a handsome spotted pony no longer, but a magnificent magic pony with a noble head and proudly arched neck. Sunshine gleamed

on his cream coat, flowing golden mane
and tail, and the gold-feathered wings
springing from his shoulders.

'Comet!' Jess gasped. She had almost
forgotten how beautiful he was. 'Are . . .
are you leaving right now?'

Comet's deep violet eyes softened with
affection. 'I must if I am to catch Destiny
and take her home safely.'

Jess's heart ached with sadness, but she
knew she was going to have to be strong
and let him go. 'I hope you and Destiny
get back to Rainbow Mist Island safely.
I'll never forget you,' she said, swallowing
her tears.

Comet spread his magnificent wings. 'I
will not forget you either. You have been
a good friend. Farewell, Jess. Ride well
and true,' he said in a deep musical voice.

Jess rushed forward, threw her arms round his silky neck and pressed her face to his glowing warmth. Comet allowed her to hug him one last time and then he slowly backed away.

There was a final flash of violet light and a silent burst of rainbow sparks, which sprinkled down around Jess in crystal jewels that dissolved with a chiming sound as they hit the ground.

Comet soared upwards. He faded and was gone.

Jess stood there, feeling empty. She could hardly believe that this had happened so fast.

Something glittered on the ground. It was a single shimmering gold wing-feather. As Jess bent and picked it up, it tingled against her palm before fading to a cream colour. She put it in her pocket, knowing that she would treasure it always as a reminder of her wonderful magic friend and the adventure they'd shared.

After a moment, she took a deep breath and prepared to face what was waiting for her. Comet had been so brave and fearless, and remembering that gave her courage. She started walking round to the front of the stable and almost bumped into Mai and Ellen.

'Jess! It's brilliant news!' cried Mai. 'Our dads think it's a great idea to use that field for the circus site.'

'So does my mum!' Ellen said, her face glowing. 'They've all gone into the house to sort out the details. Now we'll be able to extend the stables and offer all sorts of stuff, like indoor schooling and maybe

even bareback riding! Isn't it great?'

'And there's something else,' Mai said.
'When the circus is on the new site, your
dad says you can have a pony of your
own. He'll even pay for it to live at the
riding stable!'

Jess blinked in amazement. 'But how
did you know I wanted one?'

Mai grinned at her. 'Did you think I
didn't know why you kept talking to that
spotted carousel pony, when you thought

no one was looking? You've wanted a
pony for ages, haven't you?'

Jess felt a delighted smile rising up
from somewhere deep inside her as she
linked arms with Mai and Ellen. There
were some brilliant times ahead for all of
them! And none of this would have been
possible if a magic pony hadn't chosen
her to be his friend.

'Take care, Comet. Good luck,
wherever you are. And give my love to
Destiny!' she whispered to herself.

Out Now

puffin.co.uk

Magic Ponies

A New Friend

A Special Wish

A Twinkle of Hooves

Showjumping Dreams

Seaside Summer

Riding Rescue

Winter Wonderland

Pony Camp

Coming Soon

Could you be a little reindeer's special friend?

Magic Reindeer

A Christmas Wish

SUE BENTLEY

puffin.co.uk

Win a Magic Ponies goody bag!

Golden feathers from Comet's wings are falling out as he
desperately tries to find his twin sister, Destiny, who is still lost
in our world! The feathers carry a secret message for Destiny.

Two words from the message can be found in magic golden feathers
hidden in *Seaside Summer* and *Riding Rescue*.

To help save Destiny from danger, find the hidden words and put them
together to complete the message. Send it in to us and each month we
will put every correct message in a draw and pick out one lucky winner
to receive a whole stable of Magic Ponies goodies!

Send your secret message, name and address on a postcard to:

Magic Ponies competition

Puffin Books

80 Strand

London WC2R 0RL

Please help Comet save his sister!

Good luck!

puffin.co.uk

It all started with a Scarecrow

Puffin is well over sixty years old.
Sounds ancient, doesn't it? But Puffin has never been
so lively. We're always on the lookout for the next big
idea, which is how it began all those years ago.

Penguin Books was a big idea from the mind of
a man called Allen Lane, who in 1935 invented
the quality paperback and changed the world.
**And from great Penguins, great Puffins grew,
changing the face of children's books forever.**

The first four Puffin Picture Books were hatched in 1940 and the
first Puffin story book featured a man with broomstick arms called
Worzel Gummidge. In 1967 Kaye Webb, Puffin Editor, started the
Puffin Club, promising to **'make children into readers'.**
She kept that promise and over 200,000 children became
devoted Puffineers through their quarterly installments of
Puffin Post, which is now back for a new generation.

Many years from now, we hope you'll look back and
remember Puffin with a smile. **No matter what your age
or what you're into, there's a Puffin for everyone.**
The possibilities are endless, but one thing is for sure:
whether it's a picture book or a paperback, a sticker book
or a hardback, **if it's got that little Puffin
on it – it's bound to be good.**